SUPER
GAME BOY!!

SUPER
RABBIT
BOY LAND 4

SUPER FUNSTON

SUPER RABBIT BOY LAND 4

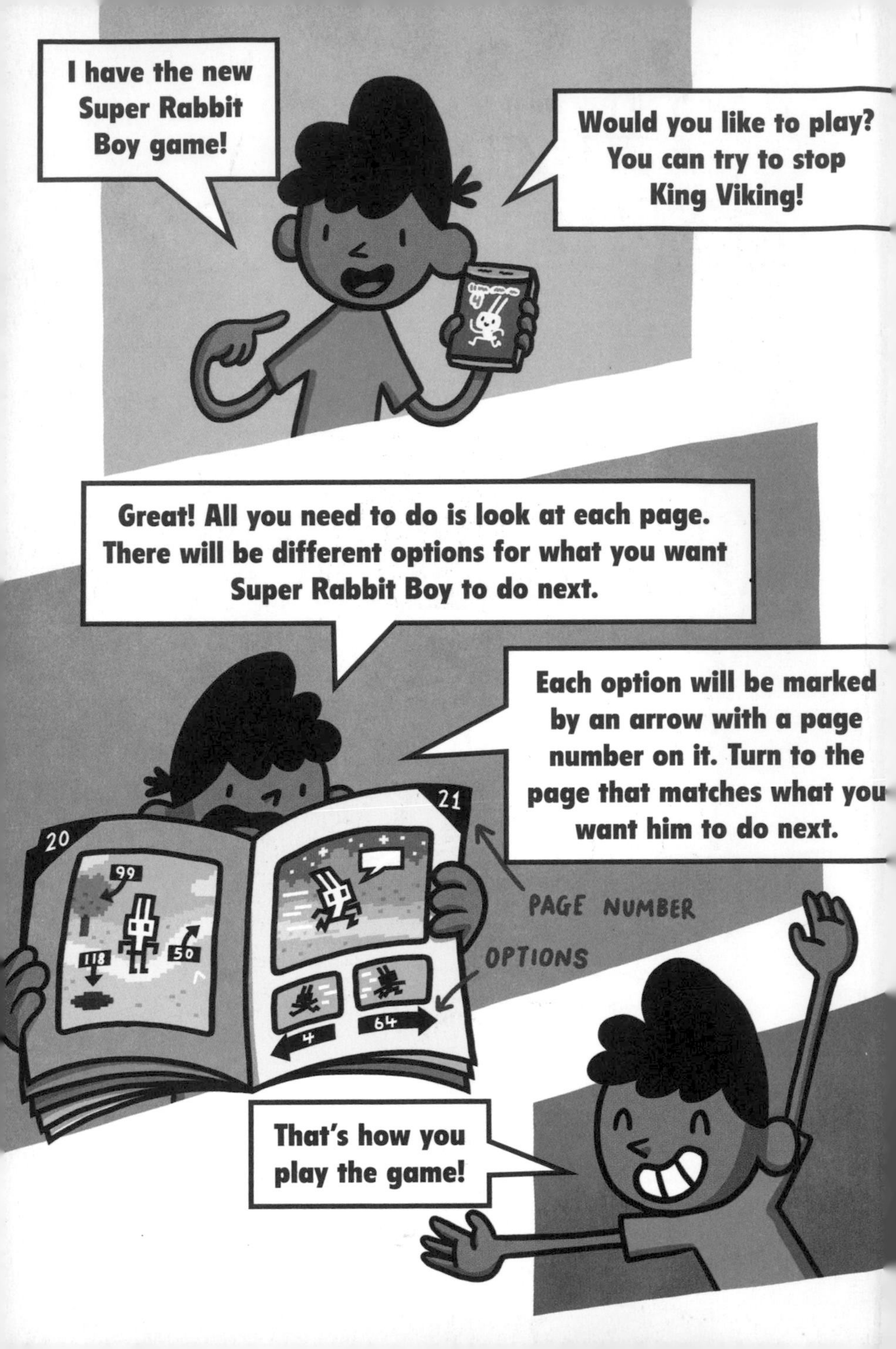
I have the new Super Rabbit Boy game!
Would you like to play? You can try to stop King Viking!
Great! All you need to do is look at each page. There will be different options for what you want Super Rabbit Boy to do next.
Each option will be marked by an arrow with a page number on it. Turn to the page that matches what you want him to do next.
PAGE NUMBER
OPTIONS
That's how you play the game!

Ready? If you want to play, then press Start!

SUPER
RABBIT
BOY LAND
4
PRESS START

START
SELECT

Choose this option to start the game!

Or choose this option if you don't want to play!

START
SELECT

START
SELECT

TURN TO PAGE 35

TURN TO PAGE 17

Super Rabbit Boy has to save his friends.
He jumps into action.

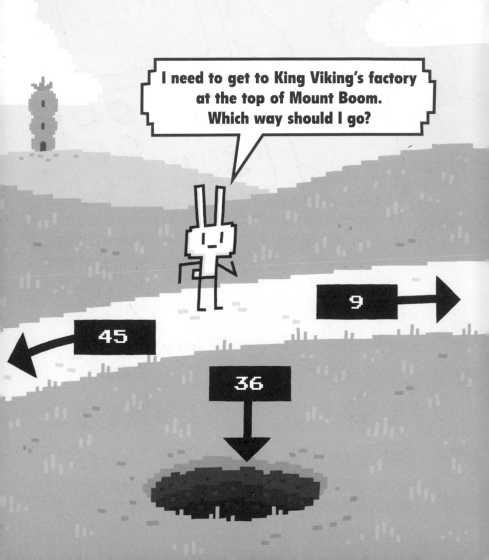

Super Rabbit Boy is in a grassy area.

Super Rabbit Boy is on a beach. He can see Mount Boom across the sea. He spots a bell nearby.

TURN TO PAGE 11

TURN TO PAGE 65

Super Rabbit Boy is deep underground.

Super Rabbit Boy starts climbing up Mount Boom. The path ahead splits in two.

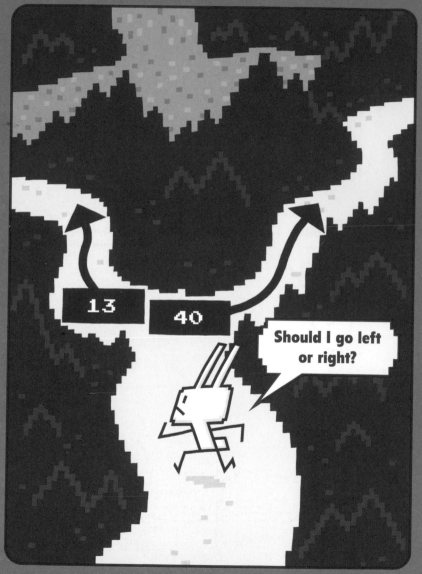

Super Rabbit Boy is finally inside King Viking's factory. Boom Boom Factory is a maze of doors and hallways.

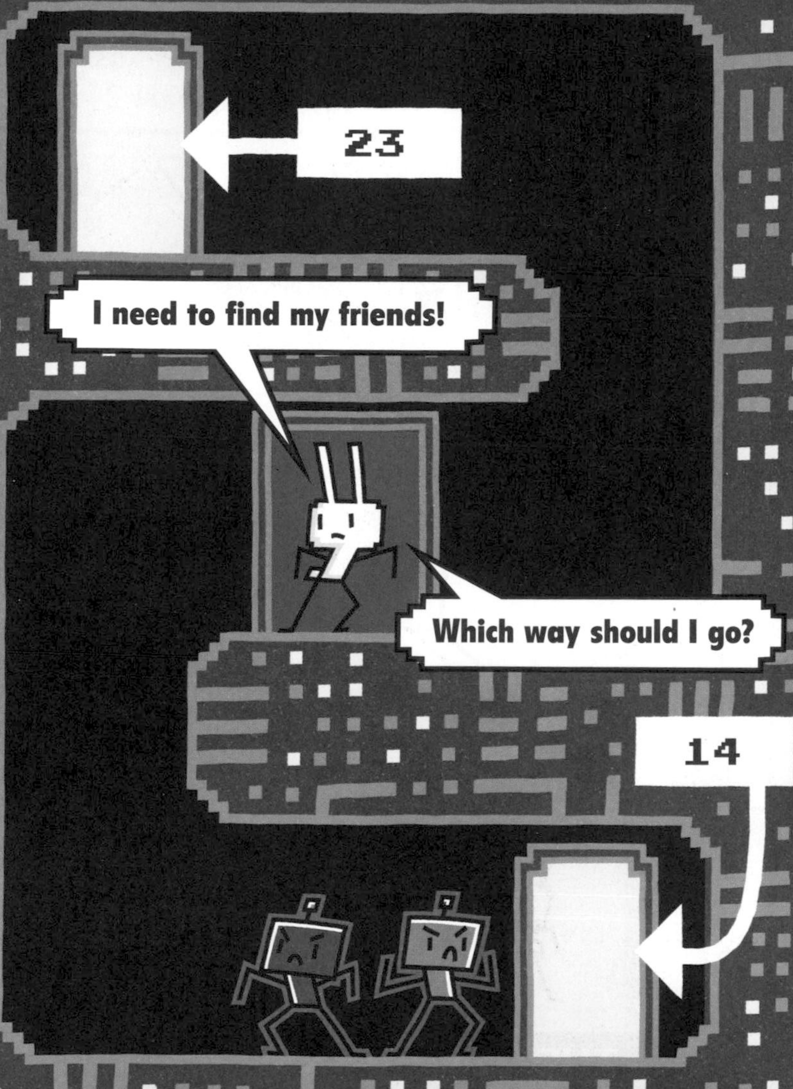
23
I need to find my friends!
Which way should I go?
14

Super Rabbit Boy finally finds King Viking.

TURN TO PAGE 15

Super Rabbit Boy steps through the door and enters a strange place. There are many doors to choose from.

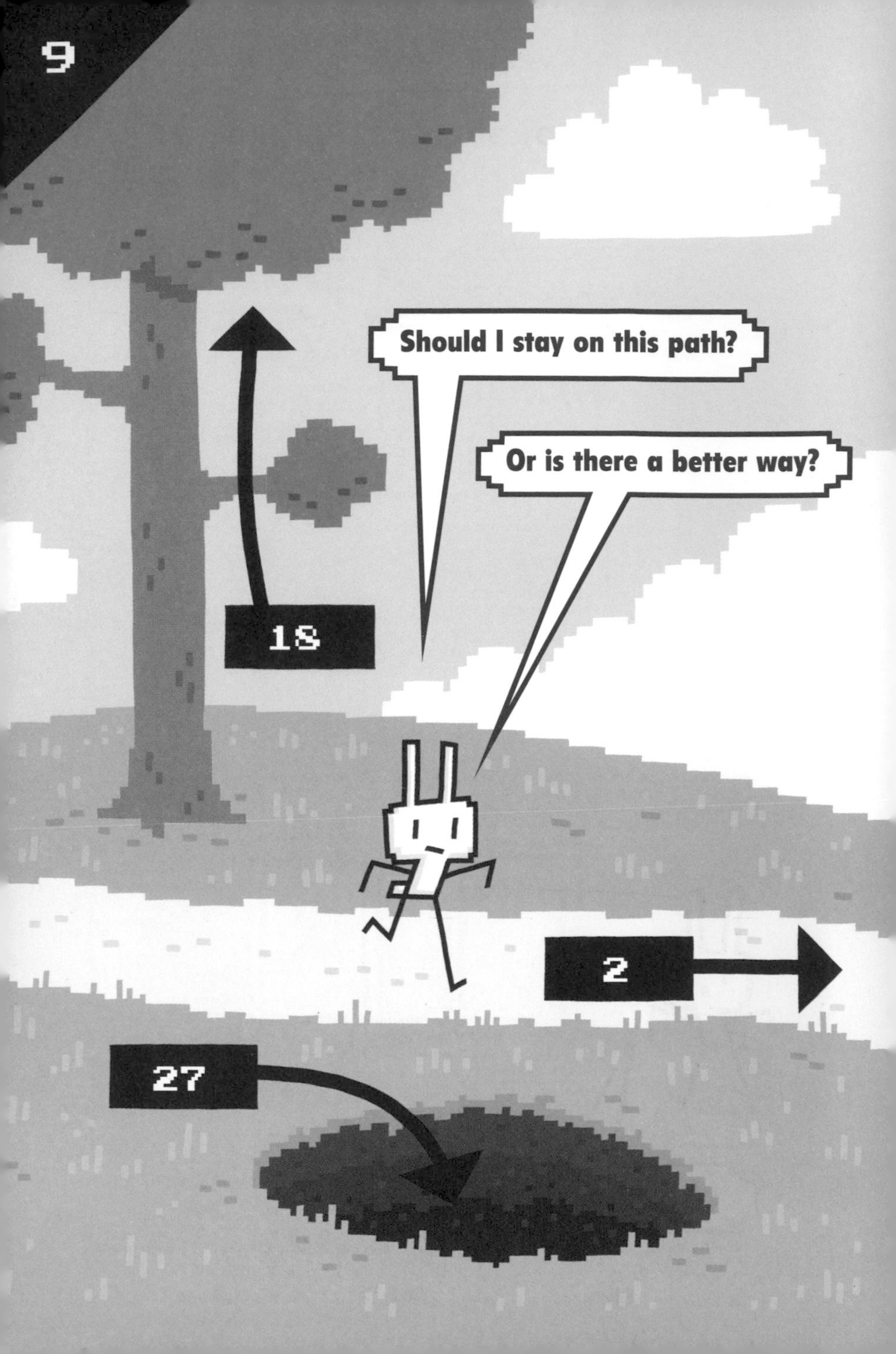
Should I stay on this path?
Or is there a better way?
18
2
27

Super Rabbit Boy takes a look at a nearby hedge.

TURN TO PAGE 2

When Super Rabbit Boy rings the bell, a whale appears.

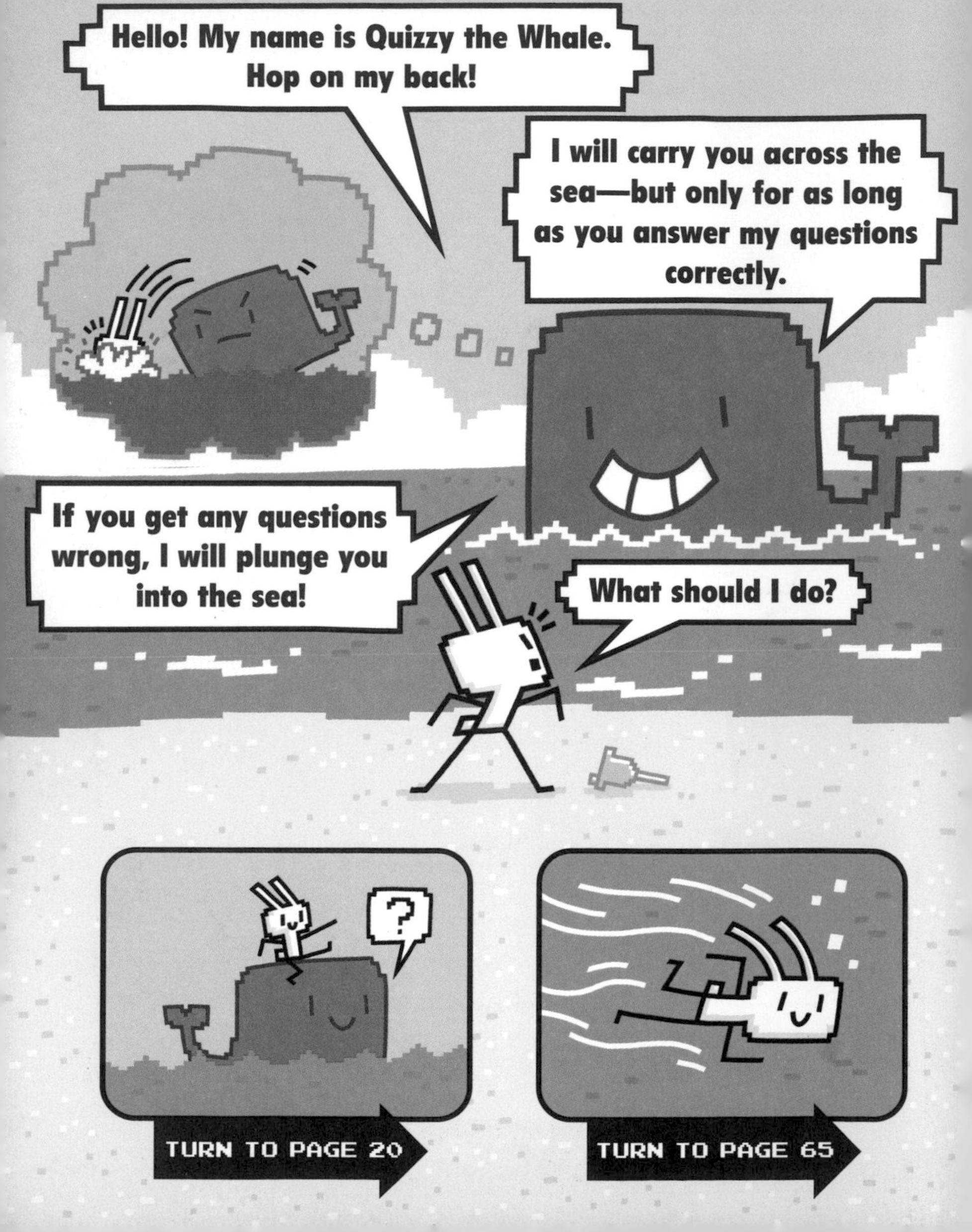
Hello! My name is Quizzy the Whale. Hop on my back!
I will carry you across the sea—but only for as long as you answer my questions correctly.
If you get any questions wrong, I will plunge you into the sea!
What should I do?
?

TURN TO PAGE 20

TURN TO PAGE 65

Super Rabbit Boy finds one of King Viking's Robo-Snakes blocking a tunnel entrance.

Super Rabbit Boy arrives outside King Viking's factory. Robots charge toward him.

TURN TO PAGE 22

TURN TO PAGE 31

Super Rabbit Boy sees some of King Viking's robots guarding a door. He tries to use his Super Jump, but the ceiling is too low.

BEEP! Without your Super Jump, you can't stop us.

BOOP! But we can stop you!

Oh bloop!

GAME OVER!
TURN TO PAGE 6 TO TRY AGAIN.

King Viking and the Robo-Boss jump into battle. The Robo-Boss's fist zooms toward Super Rabbit Boy.

I need to think fast! Should I dodge or attack?

TURN TO PAGE 24

TURN TO PAGE 33

TURN TO PAGE 42

Super Rabbit Boy is in a magical place.
There is a power up floating above him.

TURN TO PAGE 26

TURN TO PAGE 35

Super Rabbit Boy climbs to the top of the tree. He can see Mount Boom in the distance.

I can see which way to go now. I need to climb back down and follow the path!

KING VIKING'S FACTORY

MOUNT BOOM

SPLISH SPLASH SEA

WOODY WOODS

9

Super Rabbit Boy uses his Super Jump to start climbing up the floating platforms.

TURN TO PAGE 29

TURN TO PAGE 74

Hey, meanie! Can you please move out of the way?

BEEEEEEP!

TURN TO PAGE 94

TURN TO PAGE 103

Super Rabbit Boy runs past the robots and through the factory door.

TURN TO PAGE 6

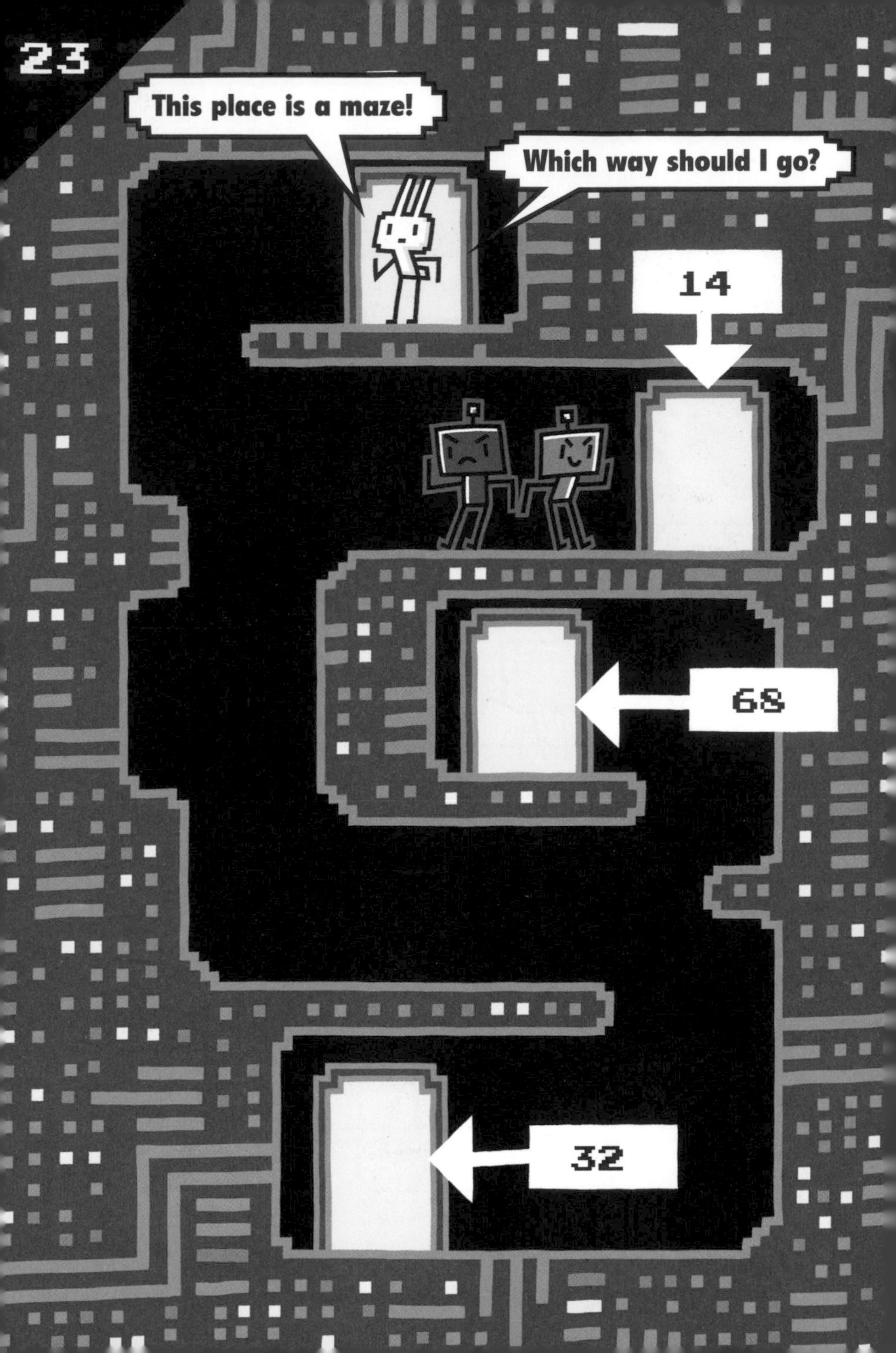
This place is a maze!
Which way should I go?
14
68
32

Super Rabbit Boy dodges the Robo-Boss,
but it's already swinging its fist again.

TURN TO
PAGE 15

TURN TO
PAGE 33

TURN TO
PAGE 42

At King Viking's factory, Super Rabbit Boy's friends are still waiting to be saved.

Suddenly, the factory starts to shake.

TURN TO PAGE 34

GAME OVER!
TURN TO PAGE 17 TO TRY AGAIN.

Super Rabbit Boy jumps into the hole. It isn't very deep.

Super Rabbit Boy tries to use his Super Jump. This time, the Robo-Boss grabs him.

GAME OVER!
TURN TO PAGE 92 TO TRY AGAIN.

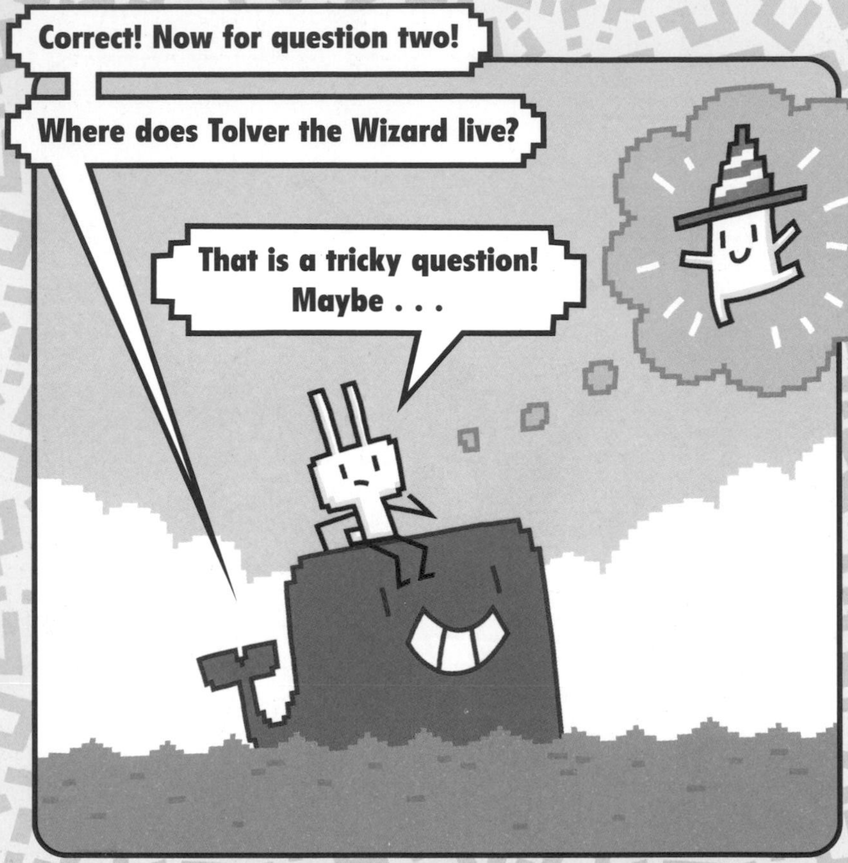
Correct! Now for question two!
Where does Tolver the Wizard live?
That is a tricky question! Maybe . . .

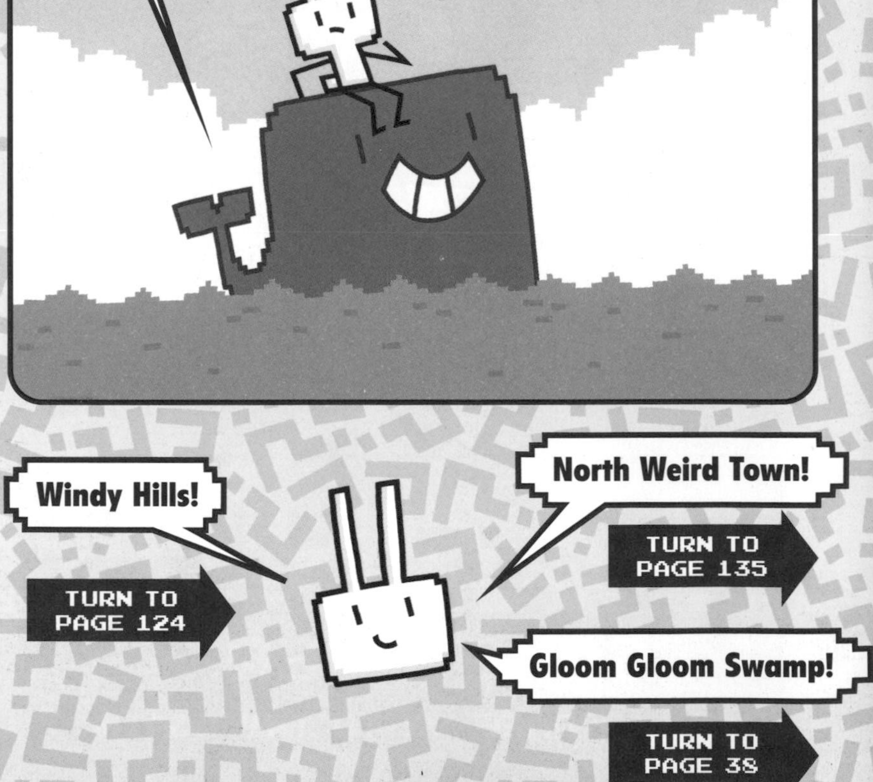
Windy Hills!
North Weird Town!
Gloom Gloom Swamp!

Windy Hills! — TURN TO PAGE 124
North Weird Town! — TURN TO PAGE 135
Gloom Gloom Swamp! — TURN TO PAGE 38

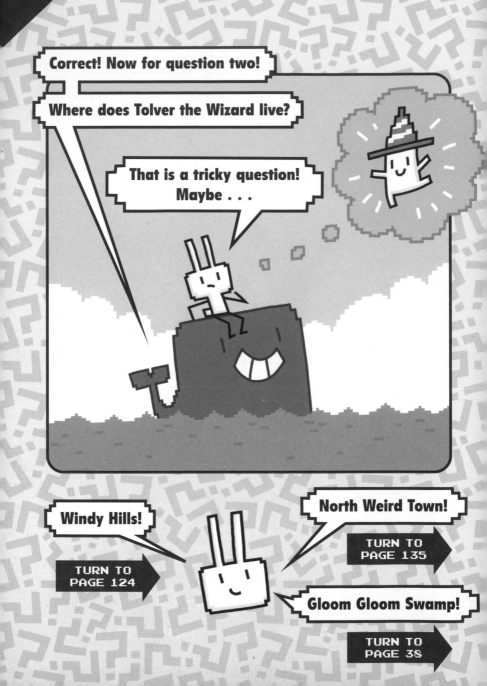

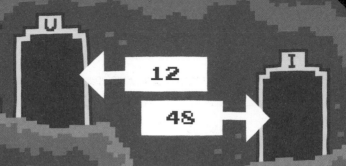

Should I go through one of these tunnels?

Or should I open the yellow door?

39

Super Rabbit Boy uses his Super Jump to break all the robots.

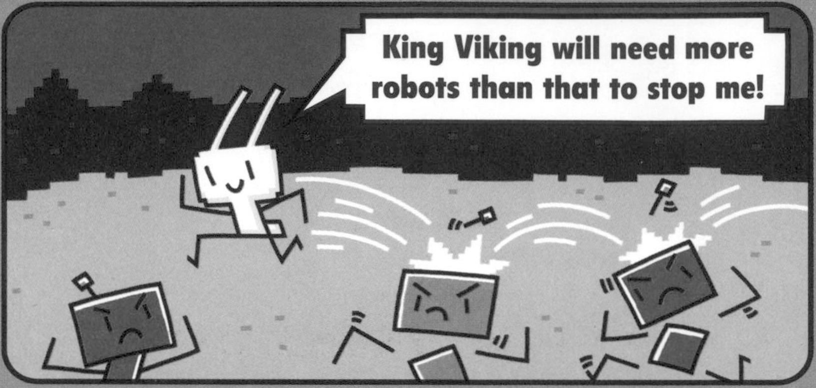
King Viking will need more robots than that to stop me!

An alarm goes off inside the factory.

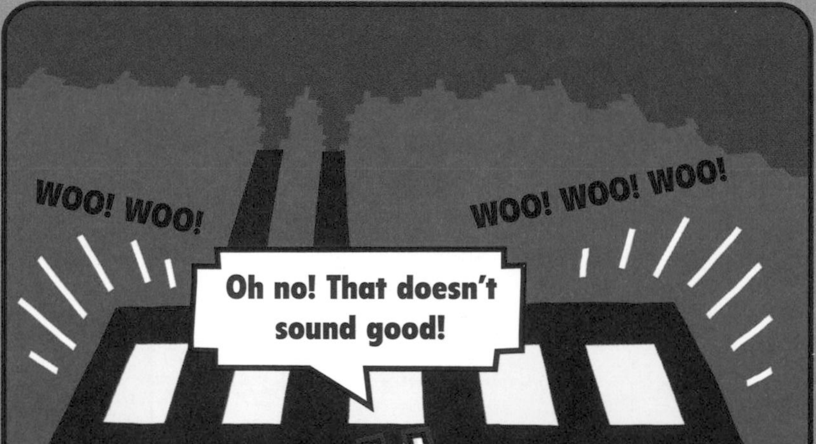
WOO! WOO!
WOO! WOO! WOO!
Oh no! That doesn't sound good!

TURN TO PAGE 49

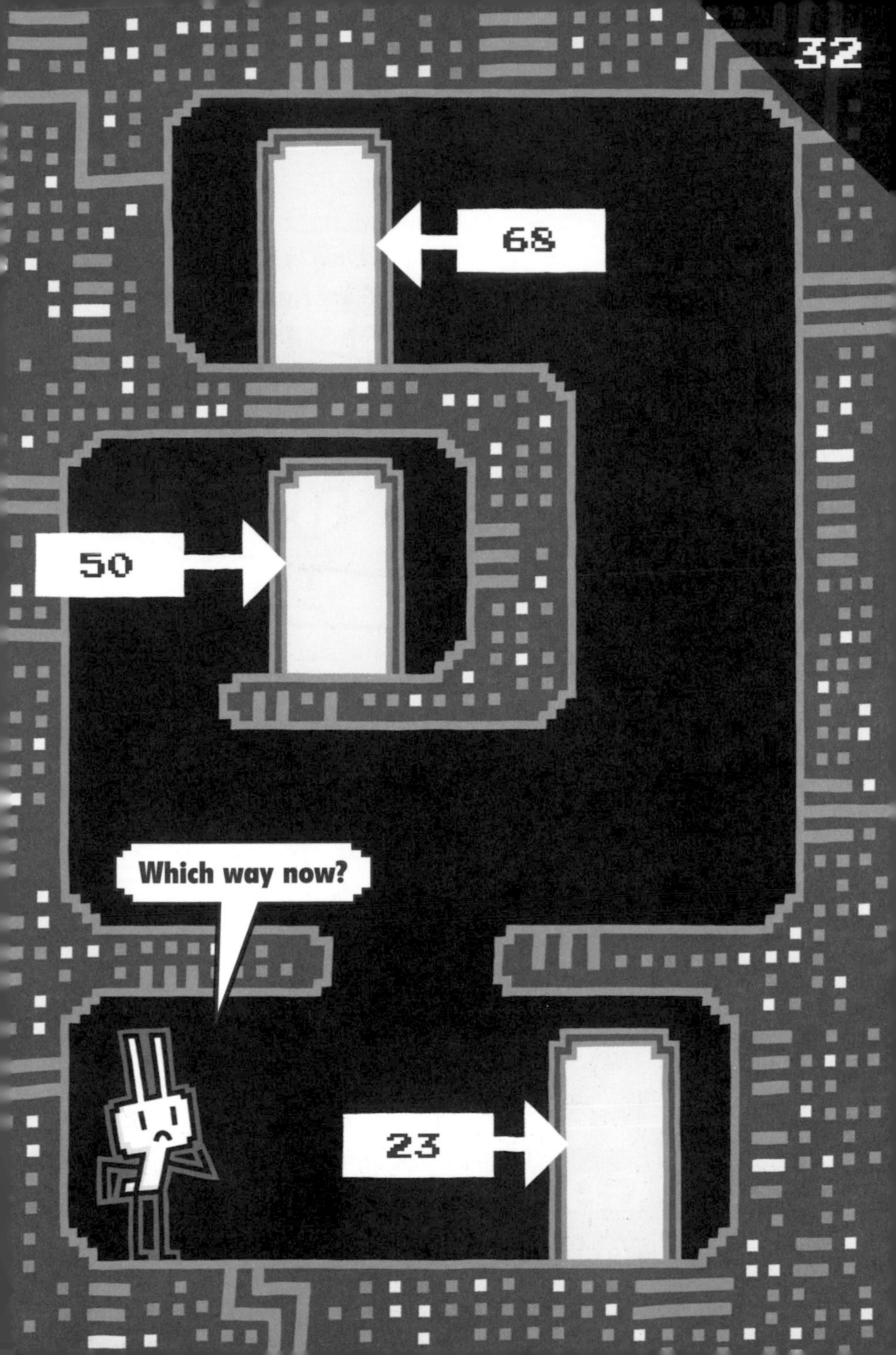
68
50
Which way now?
23

The Robo-Boss dodges Super Rabbit Boy's Super Jump and grabs him.

A giant-sized Super Rabbit Boy towers over Boom Boom Factory. He has taken the factory's roof off!

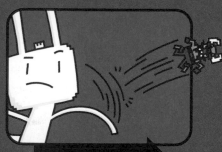

TURN TO PAGE 43

TURN TO PAGE 52

It is early morning and Super Rabbit Boy is asleep inside Carrot Castle. He is woken up by a noise outside his window.

What should Super Rabbit Boy do next?

TURN TO PAGE 44

TURN TO PAGE 53

Super Rabbit Boy jumps into the hole. It is <u>really</u> deep!

Oh bloop! Even with my Super Jump I can't get out of here.

I'm stuck!

GAME OVER!
TURN TO PAGE 1 TO TRY AGAIN.

Super Rabbit Boy has made it to the highest platform.

Should I get inside this cannon?

Or maybe I should just jump back down.

TURN TO PAGE 46

TURN TO PAGE 114

Correct! It's time for question three!

If a train leaves Animal Town at the same time as a train leaves Elf Town, how long would it take for them to pass?

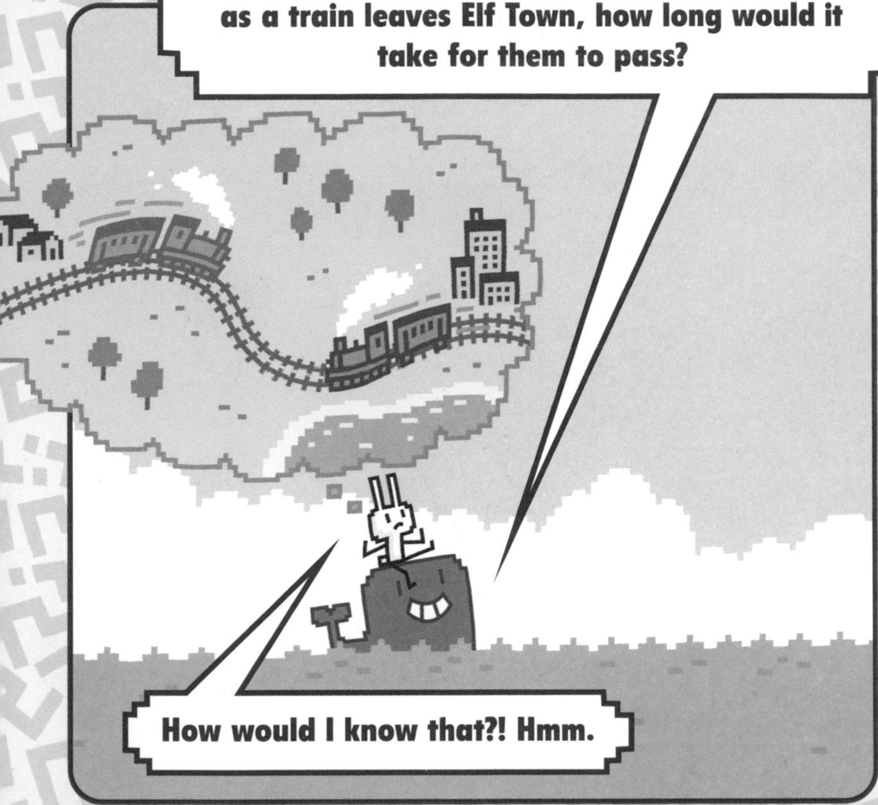

One hour?

TURN TO PAGE 93

There isn't a train station in Animal Town!

TURN TO PAGE 56

Two days.

TURN TO PAGE 139

I don't know!

TURN TO PAGE 47

Super Rabbit Boy steps through the door. He is suddenly in a strange place. There are scary, noisy carrots everywhere! There is no way back.

CARROTS!

CARROTS!

Oh bloop! I should have stayed in bed this morning!

CAAAAARRRRROOOOTTS!

GAME OVER!
TURN TO PAGE 30 TO TRY AGAIN.

Super Rabbit Boy is almost at the factory.
There are robots guarding the front door.

TURN TO PAGE 31

TURN TO PAGE 132

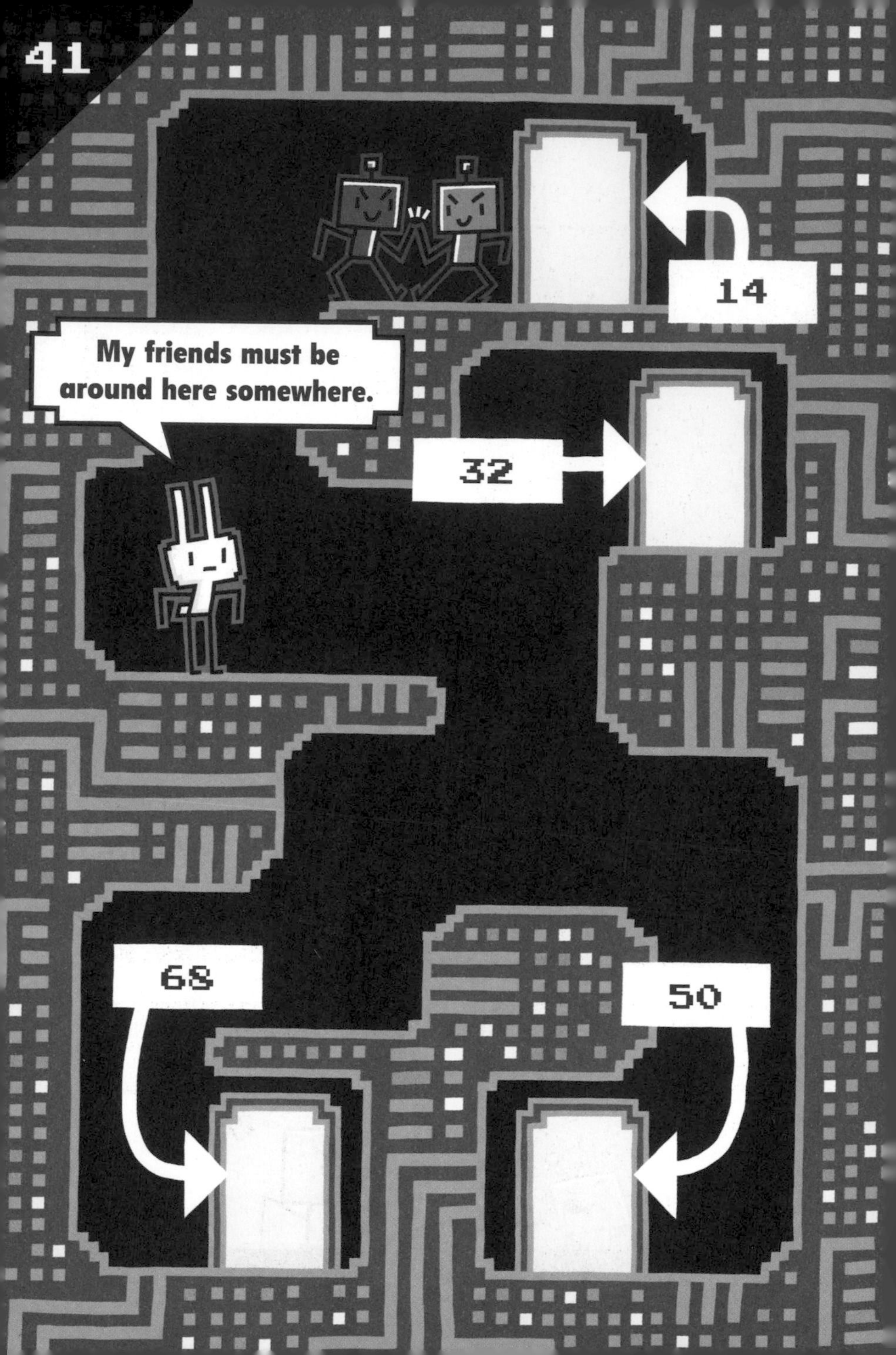

14
My friends must be around here somewhere.
32
68
50

Super Rabbit Boy jumps away from the Robo-Boss and lands next to a pillar. The Robo-Boss is already coming at him with another punch.

Ha! We'll get you this time!

TURN TO PAGE 33

TURN TO PAGE 51

Super Rabbit Boy easily throws King Viking into the distance.

Wah! You giant stinker!

Let's get you all home!

Thank you! You've been a massive help!

You did an amazing job! I've never seen that ending before!

THE END! YOU WIN!

Super Rabbit Boy goes back to sleep. He has a bad dream about scary, noisy carrots!

GAME OVER!
TURN TO PAGE 35 TO TRY AGAIN

Super Rabbit Boy arrives in Animal Town. It is completely deserted.

As soon as Super Rabbit Boy climbs into the cannon, it goes off with a big bang! He is blasted up into the sky.

Boing! Boing! Here I go!

TURN TO PAGE 99 ➡

Quizzy blasts Super Rabbit Boy into the air with his waterspout!

TURN TO PAGE 99

Super Rabbit Boy spots his friend Mega Mole Girl.

Robots come running out of the factory. Super Rabbit Boy is quickly surrounded.

Oh bloop! What should I do?

TURN TO PAGE 22

TURN TO PAGE 67

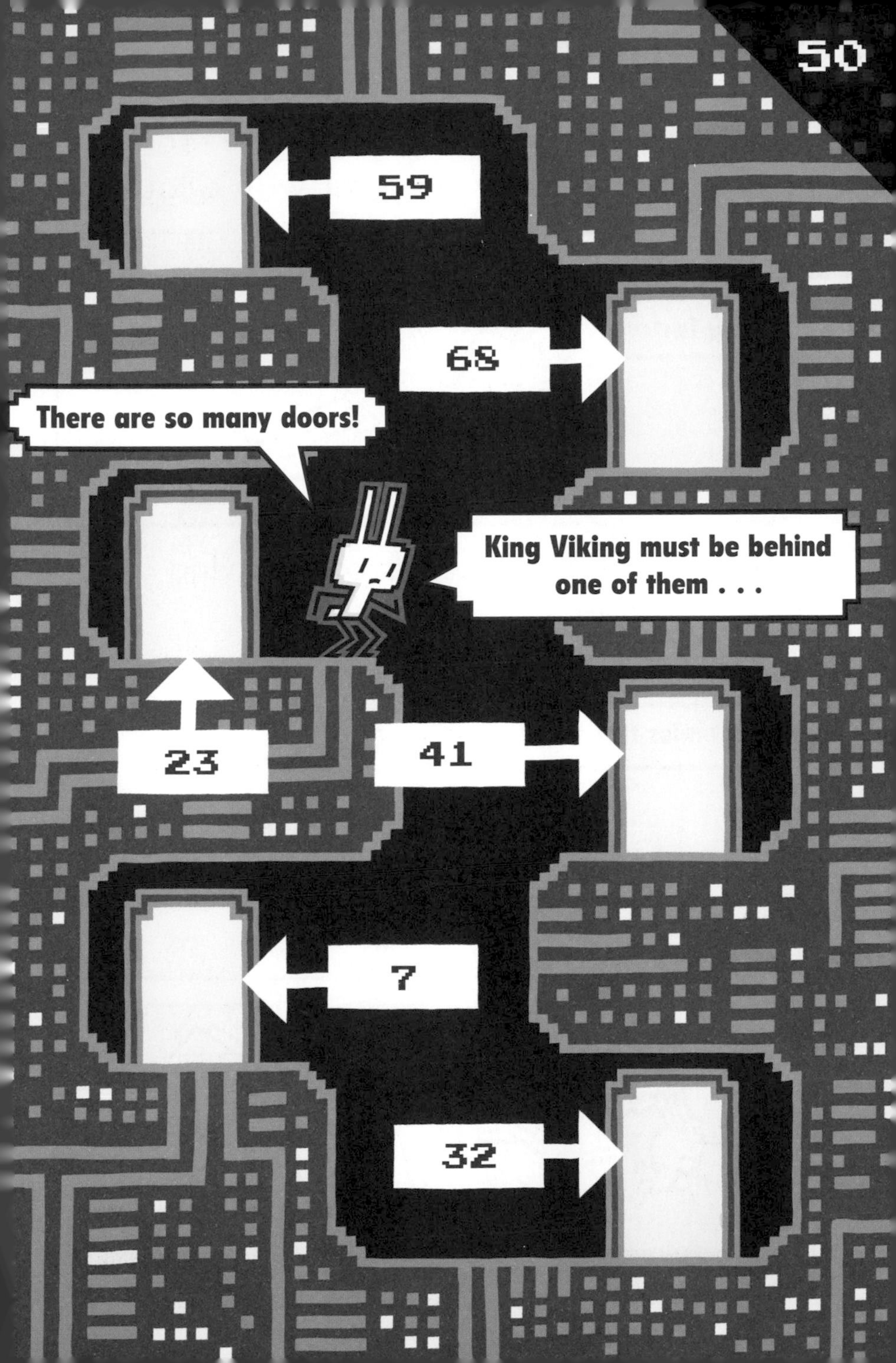
59
68
There are so many doors!
King Viking must be behind one of them . . .
23
41
7
32

Super Rabbit Boy dodges quickly. The Robo-Boss punches the pillar with a loud crash.

The Robo-Boss takes another swing at Super Rabbit Boy.

TURN TO PAGE 79

TURN TO PAGE 69

TURN TO PAGE 60

While Super Rabbit Boy is laughing at King Viking, a robot sneaks toward his power up crown.

The robot grabs the power up! Super Rabbit Boy shrinks back to normal size.

TURN TO PAGE 61

Super Rabbit Boy looks out the window. He can see three of King Viking's robots outside.

What are they up to?

TURN TO PAGE 62

TURN TO PAGE 71

Super Rabbit Boy looks behind a bush. He is surprised when King Viking's robots leap out!

TURN TO PAGE 1

TURN TO PAGE 63

Super Rabbit Boy jumps back down to the ground. He lands in the woods.

TURN TO PAGE 92

Super Rabbit Boy jumps onto the shore.

TURN TO PAGE 133

The Robo-Boss finds Super Rabbit Boy
hiding inside the hedge and grabs him.

GAME OVER!

TURN TO PAGE 126 TO TRY AGAIN.

Super Rabbit Boy jumps out from the hedge.

TURN TO PAGE 77

TURN TO PAGE 134

BAM! As soon as Super Rabbit Boy steps through the door, it slams shut behind him. He is trapped!

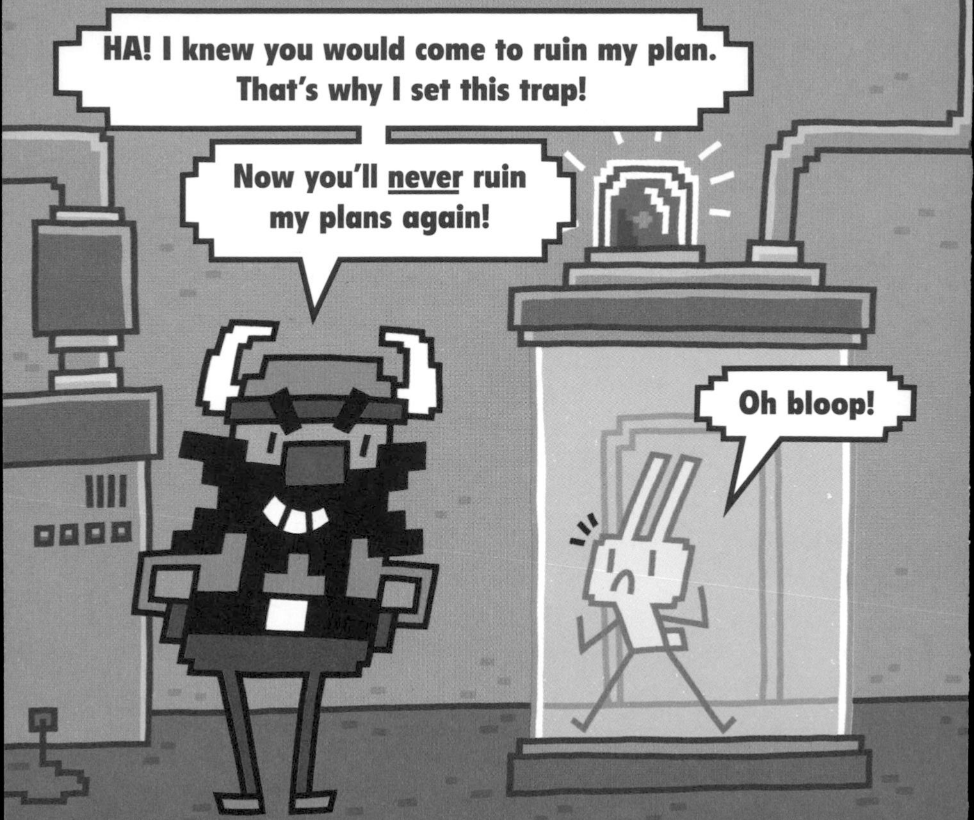

GAME OVER!

TURN TO PAGE 6 TO TRY AGAIN.

Super Rabbit Boy manages to dodge again. The Robo-Boss is already striking toward him once more.

TURN TO PAGE 69

TURN TO PAGE 79

A giant-sized King Viking towers over Super Rabbit Boy.

Now YOU are the one in BIG trouble!

Oh bloop!

GAME OVER!
TURN TO PAGE 8 TO TRY AGAIN.

Super Rabbit Boy calls out to the robots.

What should Super Rabbit Boy do next?

TURN TO PAGE 44

TURN TO PAGE 71

Super Rabbit Boy easily defeats the robots.

TURN TO PAGE 45

Super Rabbit Boy uses his Super Jump to start climbing up the floating platforms. The Robo-Boss cannot reach him.

TURN TO PAGE 37

TURN TO PAGE 109

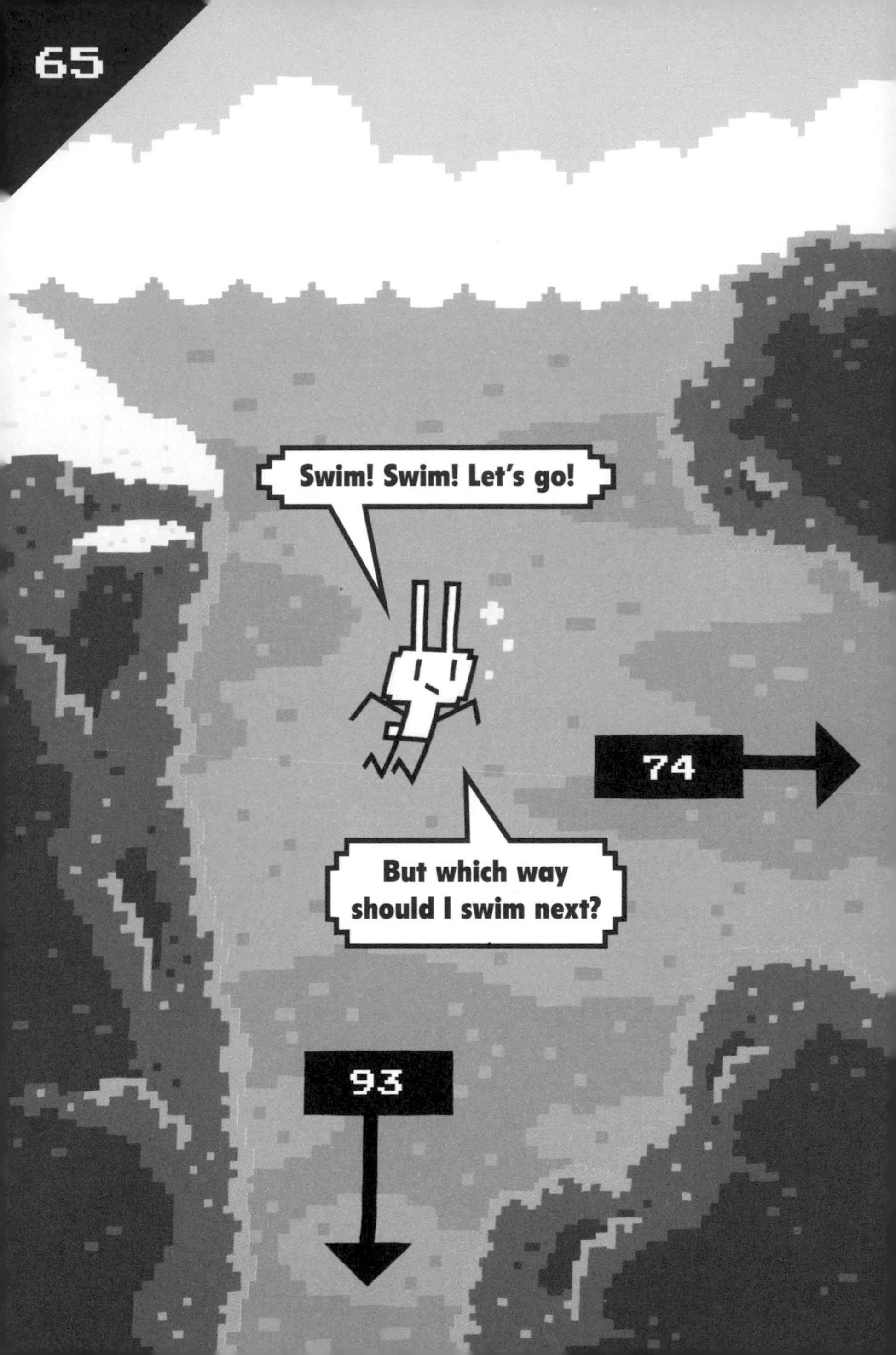
Swim! Swim! Let's go!
But which way should I swim next?
74
93

Super Rabbit Boy still can't find the exit.
He asks a stranger for help.

Super Rabbit Boy uses his Super Jump to stop the robots. But more robots stream out of the factory.

TURN TO PAGE 76

TURN TO PAGE 86

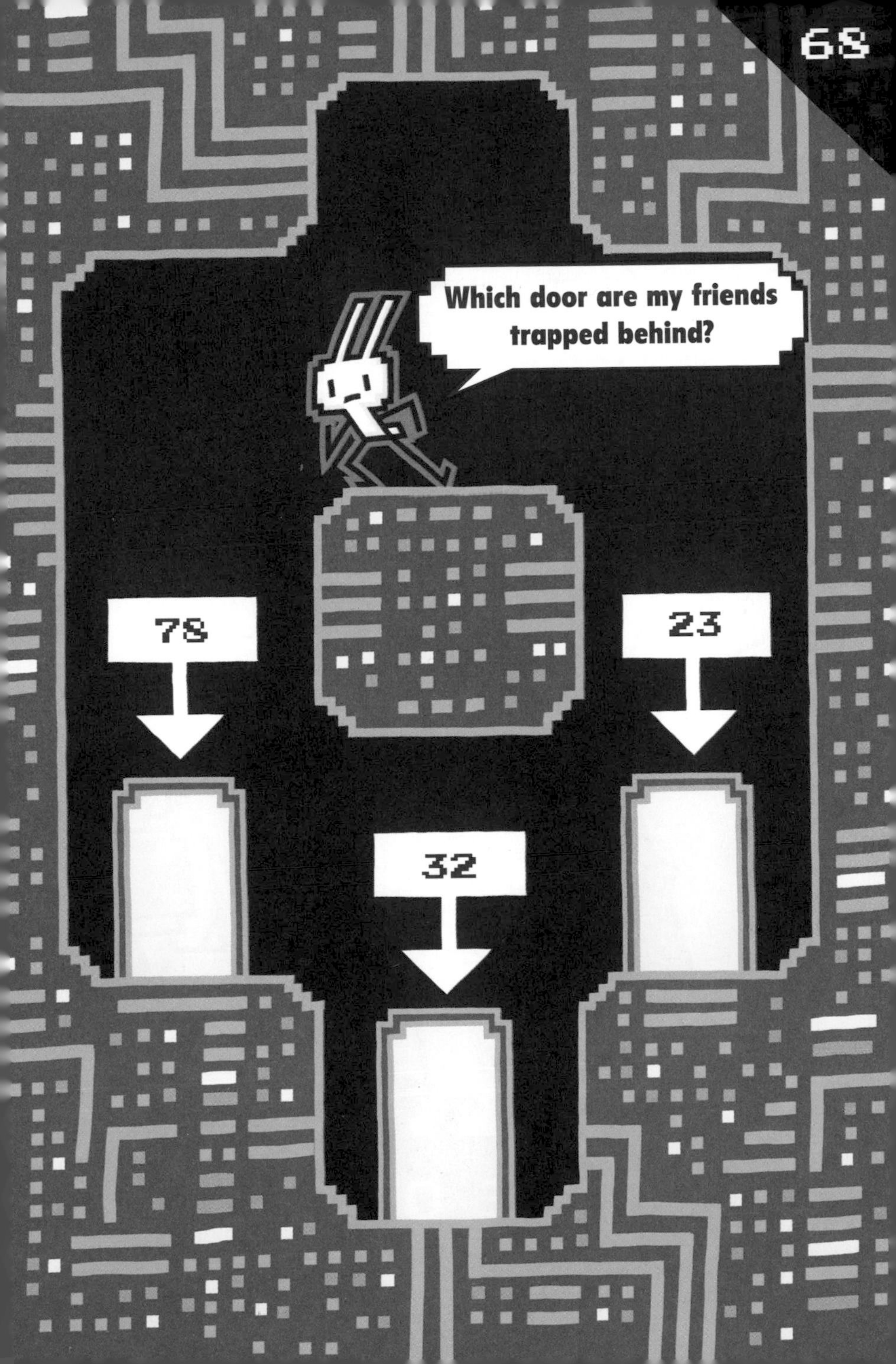
Which door are my friends trapped behind?
78
23
32

Super Rabbit Boy tries to use his Super Jump against the Robo-Boss. It doesn't work! The Robo-Boss snatches him out of the air.

Ha! My Robo-Boss is too strong for you!

You'll never stop it with your super-weak Super Jump!

Oh bloop!

GAME OVER!

TURN TO PAGE 7 TO TRY AGAIN.

Super Rabbit Boy is on top of a hill. There is a power up floating above the ground.

Super Rabbit Boy runs out of Carrot Castle. He is ready to chase after the robots, but they're gone!

Super Rabbit Boy searches inside one of the houses.

Super Rabbit Boy laughs. While he is busy laughing, the Robo-Boss recovers its balance. It quickly grabs Super Rabbit Boy!

GAME OVER!

TURN TO PAGE 126 TO TRY AGAIN.

Suddenly, Super Rabbit Boy is surrounded by Robo-Fish!

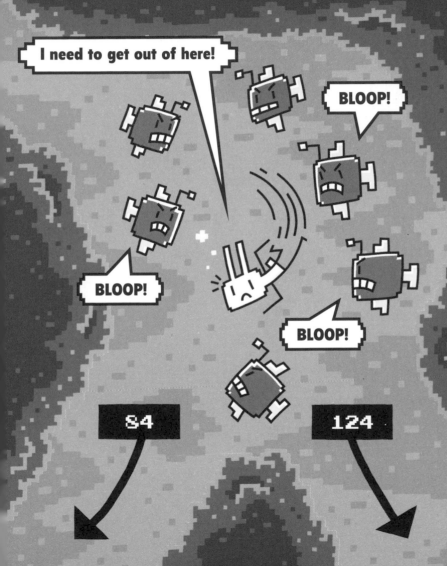

The tunnel leads Super Rabbit Boy to more tunnels.

Super Rabbit Boy is starting to get tired.

TURN TO PAGE 67

TURN TO PAGE 6

Super Rabbit Boy is falling a long way down.

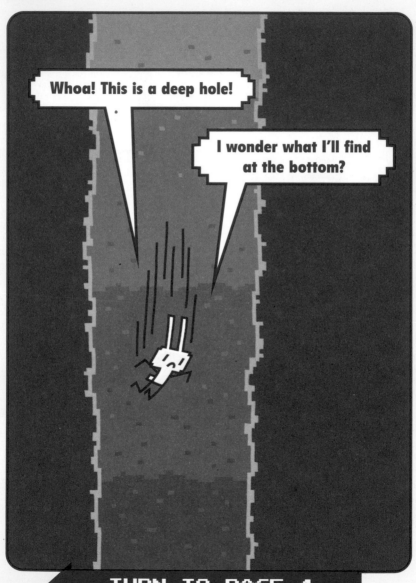

TURN TO PAGE 4

Super Rabbit Boy is in King Viking's lab!
There is no sign of King Viking.

Super Rabbit Boy avoids the Robo-Boss again.

TURN TO PAGE 69

TURN TO PAGE 89

Super Rabbit Boy grabs the power up. In a flash, he is turned into a tree!

Oh bloop!

This won't help me save my friends!

GAME OVER!

TURN TO PAGE 8 TO TRY AGAIN.

Super Rabbit Boy looks behind the hedge, but the robots aren't there. They were behind the rocks! They jump out and charge toward Super Rabbit Boy.

Oh bloop!

What should I do now?

TURN TO PAGE 100

TURN TO PAGE 110

Super Rabbit Boy sees an open book. He reads about a super secret power up hidden in a super secret place.

If I can find that power up, I'll easily defeat King Viking!

TURN TO PAGE 72

CRASH! Super Rabbit Boy lands on top of the Robo-Boss that guards the woods. The Robo-Boss is destroyed.

Ha! Thank you for breaking my fall!

BOOP! King Viking will break you for breaking me!

TURN TO PAGE 87

Super Rabbit Boy swims away from the Robo-Fish. He thinks he is finally safe when suddenly—

CHOMP!

He gets gobbled up by a GIANT Robo-Fish!

GAME OVER!

TURN TO PAGE 65 TO TRY AGAIN.

Super Rabbit Boy is sucked through the hole and finds himself in an underground cavern.

Super Rabbit Boy uses his Super Jump to stop the robots. But even more robots come running out of the factory.

More robots?! Now what should I do?

TURN TO PAGE 76

TURN TO PAGE 95

Super Rabbit Boy walks along the path through the woods.

These woods are nice when there isn't a Robo-Boss blocking my way.

The path ends. He has made it to the sea.

Watch out, King Viking! I'm getting closer!

TURN TO PAGE 3

Super Rabbit Boy is finally inside King Viking's factory. Boom Boom Factory is a maze of doors and hallways.

The Robo-Boss misses Super Rabbit Boy. It punches the second pillar with another loud crash! The whole room starts to shake and shudder.

Wah! What have you done to my factory, you stinker?!

I need to get out of here!

TURN TO PAGE 98

TURN TO PAGE 107

Super Rabbit Boy is suddenly in a room inside King Viking's factory. All of his friends are there.

GAME OVER!

TURN TO PAGE 8 TO TRY AGAIN.

Super Rabbit Boy looks behind the rocks. He spots the robots.

BEEP! Do you think he'll find us here?

BOOP! No way!

BLOOP! What should we have for dinner today?

I found them! What should I do now?

TURN TO PAGE 100

TURN TO PAGE 110

There is a Robo-Boss blocking the path through the woods.

BEEP! You won't get past me!

TURN TO PAGE 2

TURN TO PAGE 101

Super Rabbit Boy spots a sunken ship on the seafloor.

Super Rabbit Boy tries to run away. The Robo-Snake lunges at him.

SNAP!

GAME OVER!
TURN TO PAGE 4 TO TRY AGAIN.

Super Rabbit Boy uses his Super Jump to stop the robots. But robots continue to stream out of the factory.

They just keep coming! What should I do now?

TURN TO PAGE 76

TURN TO PAGE 104

The Robo-Boss has been stopped at last.

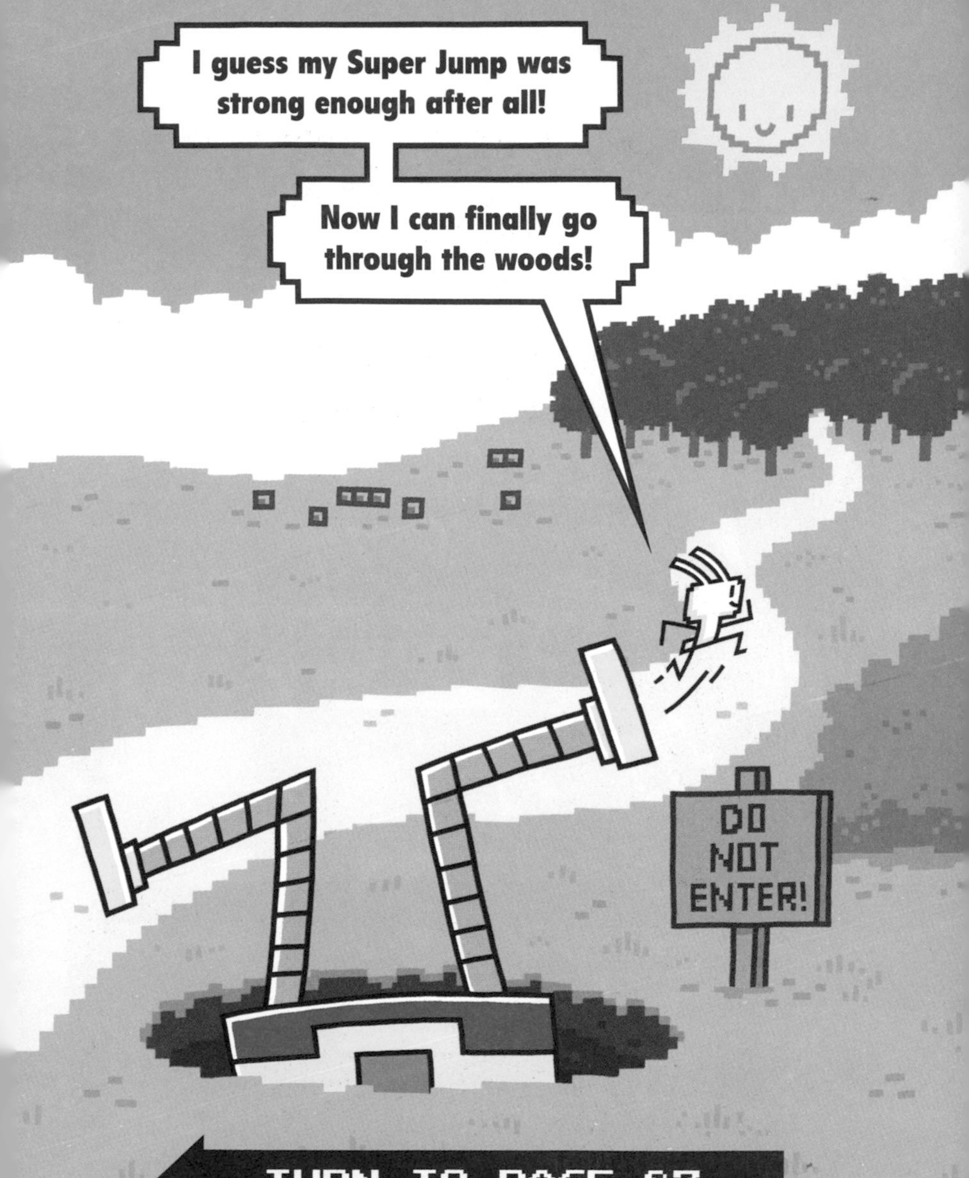

TURN TO PAGE 87

Super Rabbit Boy sees three more doors. He hears a familiar sound coming from behind one of them.

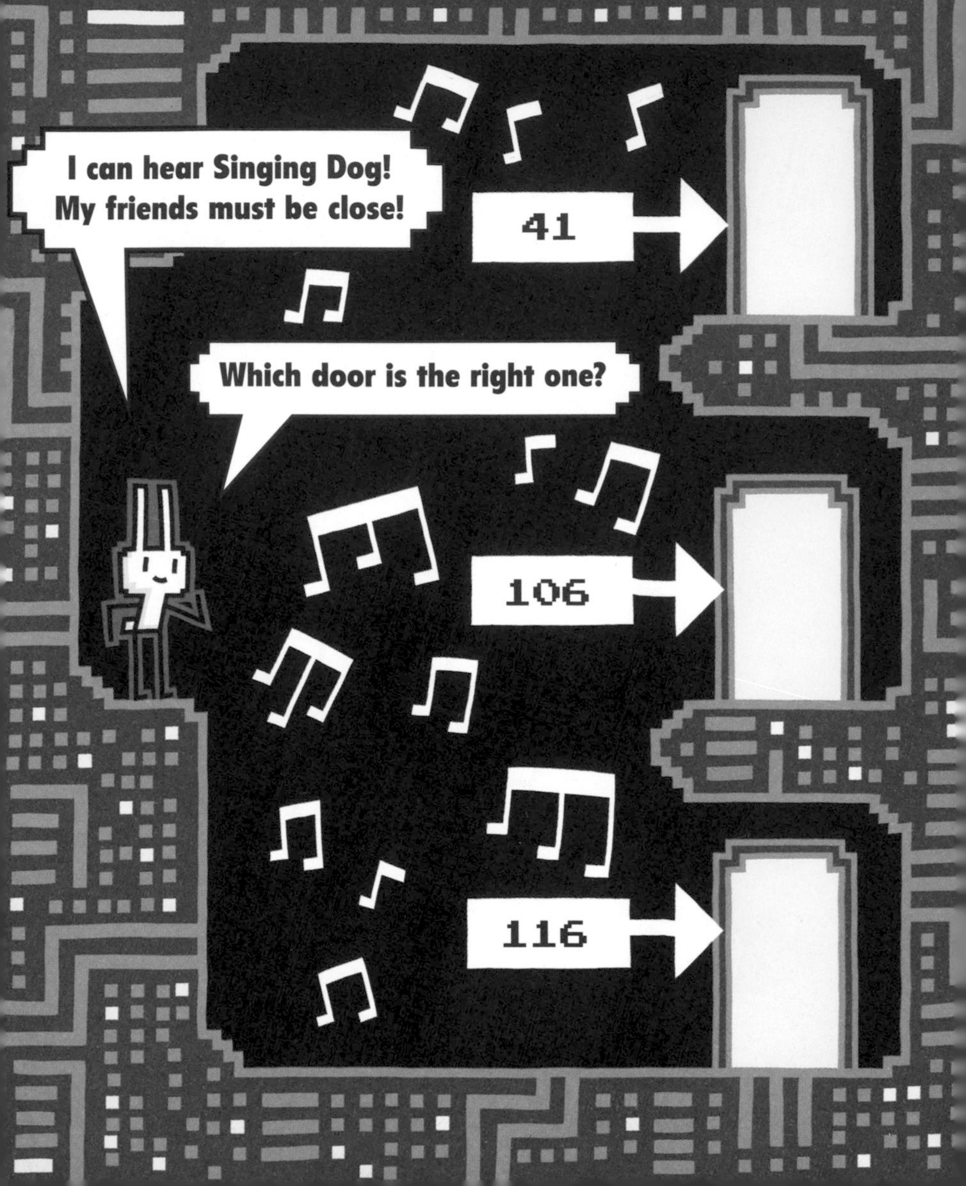
I can hear Singing Dog! My friends must be close!
41
Which door is the right one?
106
116

The factory ceiling comes crashing down. King Viking, the Robo-Boss, and Super Rabbit Boy are all caught underneath it.

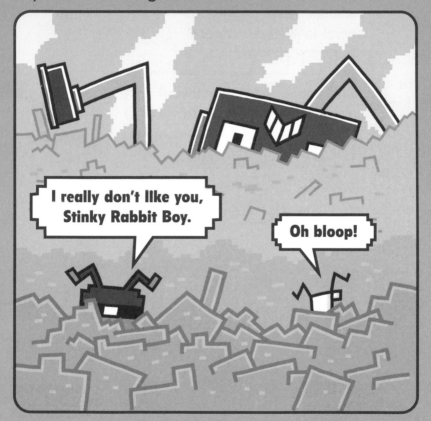

GAME OVER!

TURN TO PAGE 51 TO TRY AGAIN

Super Rabbit Boy is on a cloud high up in the sky.

Super Rabbit Boy talks to the robots.

The robots drop the letter, then run away.

Super Rabbit Boy tries to use his Super Jump to stop the Robo-Boss. But it doesn't work!

BOOP! Your Super Jump isn't strong enough to stop me!

What should I try now?

TURN TO PAGE 111

TURN TO PAGE 120

Super Rabbit Boy explores the sunken ship.

Super Rabbit Boy uses his Super Jump to dodge the Robo-Snake as it lunges forward. BAM! The Robo-Snake crashes into the wall and breaks apart.

Super Rabbit Boy uses his Super Jump to stop the robots. But more robots come running out of the factory.

Even more robots?!
Now what should I do?

TURN TO PAGE 76

TURN TO PAGE 115

Super Rabbit Boy uses his Super Jump on the wobbling Robo-Boss. The Robo-Boss tumbles backward into the big hole in the ground.

BLOOOOOPPPP!

DO NOT ENTER!

TURN TO PAGE 96

Super Rabbit Boy finds his friends! But—
SLAM! A cage crashes down on top of him.

GAME OVER!
TURN TO PAGE 88 TO TRY AGAIN.

The factory ceiling comes crashing down. But Super Rabbit Boy manages to jump through a doorway.

Super Rabbit Boy sees King Viking and the Robo-Boss trapped under the rubble.

TURN TO PAGE 140

The cannon blasts Super Rabbit Boy into outer space.

Oh bloop!

I didn't think a cannon would send me <u>this</u> far away!

GAME OVER!

TURN TO PAGE 99 TO TRY AGAIN.

Super Rabbit Boy uses his Super Jump against the Robo-Boss. It doesn't work. The Robo-Boss grabs him.

TURN TO PAGE 64 TO TRY AGAIN

Super Rabbit Boy uses his Super Jump to easily defeat the robots.

He spots a letter on the ground.

Super Rabbit Boy starts to run away. The Robo-Boss chases after him.

BEEP! You're too weak to stop me!

BOOP! Good thing King Viking built me strong enough to stop <u>you</u>!

Oh bloop!

TURN TO PAGE 126

CREAK! Super Rabbit Boy opens the treasure chest. There is no treasure inside, but there is a ghost!

Eek!

Don't be scared! I don't have any treasure, but I can give you a clue instead.

If you want to find the door to a very secret place, the password is . . . TWO DAYS!

I'm going to go back to sleep now. Good night!

Thank you, Mr. Ghost.

TURN TO PAGE 102

Super Rabbit Boy walks down a long tunnel. At last, he finds an exit—but he's back at Carrot Castle!

Oh bloop! This isn't the right exit!

I'm glad I helped my friend! If he'd taken a different exit, he would have gone straight to King Viking's horrible factory!

GAME OVER!

TURN TO PAGE 4 TO TRY AGAIN.

Super Rabbit Boy is falling a long way back down to the ground.

TURN TO PAGE 83

Super Rabbit Boy uses his Super Jump to stop the robots. He waits to see if any more come out of the factory. They don't.

Phew! I must have broken all of King Viking's robots!

Watch out, King Viking! I'm here to save the day!

Boing! Boing! Let's go!

TURN TO PAGE 88

Super Rabbit Boy finds his friends!

The cannon blasts Super Rabbit Boy onto a small island surrounded by sea monsters.

GAME OVER!

TURN TO PAGE 99 TO TRY AGAIN.

Super Rabbit Boy leaps out from the hedge. The Robo-Boss is startled and loses its balance.

TURN TO PAGE 73

TURN TO PAGE 105

DEAR <u>STINKY</u> RABBIT BOY,

THERE WILL BE NO MORE PARTIES IN ANIMAL TOWN! I HAVE KIDNAPPED ALL OF YOUR FRIENDS. I'VE HAD ENOUGH OF ALL THEIR FUN AND GAMES. YOU CAN'T HAVE ANY MORE STINKY PARTIES IF YOU DON'T HAVE ANY FRIENDS TO PARTY WITH!

SORRY, NOT SORRY.

DON'T EVEN THINK OF COMING TO MY FACTORY TO RUIN MY PLAN!

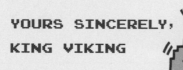

YOURS SINCERELY, KING VIKING

P.S.

I HOPE THIS MAKES YOU SAD AND YOU CRY ALL DAY.

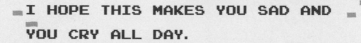
TURN TO PAGE 1

Super Rabbit Boy tries to use his Super Jump again. It still doesn't work.

BEEP! I told you! Your Super Jump isn't strong enough to stop me!

How can I stop this mean Robo-Boss?

TURN TO PAGE 28

TURN TO PAGE 111

CREAK! Super Rabbit Boy opens the door. A scary sea monster pops out!

GAME OVER!
TURN TO PAGE 93 TO TRY AGAIN.

The animals follow Super Rabbit Boy. But King Viking is waiting for them. His Robo-Boss's GIANT fist zooms straight toward Super Rabbit Boy!

I won't let you get away!

TURN TO PAGE 125

TURN TO PAGE 128

Super Rabbit Boy keeps jumping higher and higher. He is quite high up now.

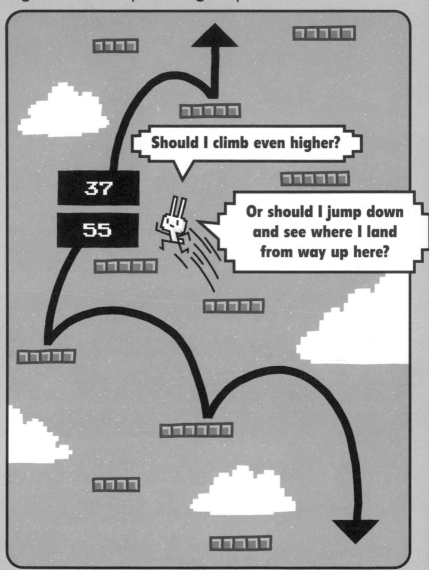

Super Rabbit Boy is in an underwater area full of crabs.

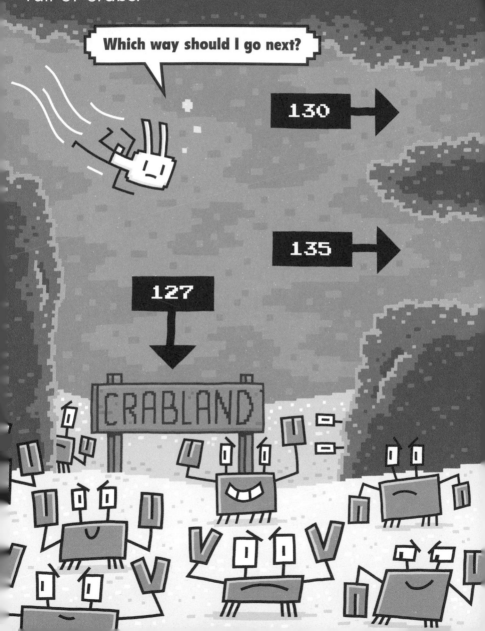

Super Rabbit Boy tries to use his Super Jump. But he is tired after fighting King Viking's robots. The Robo-Boss grabs him.

HA! I win this time, Stinky Rabbit Boy!

Oh bloop!

GAME OVER!
TURN TO PAGE 88 TO TRY AGAIN.

Super Rabbit Boy runs out of the woods, but the Robo-Boss is right behind him.

Super Rabbit Boy swims down to Crabland.
Crab Queen grabs him with her pincers!

Your first mistake was coming to Crabland.

**Your second mistake was thinking
we would let you leave!**

GAME OVER!
TURN TO PAGE 124 TO TRY AGAIN

Super Rabbit Boy dodges the Robo-Boss's giant fist as it bashes a hole in the wall.

Super Rabbit Boy looks through the hole. He has found the perfect way to escape.

TURN TO PAGE 131

Super Rabbit Boy quickly hides in a hedge. The Robo-Boss smashes some platforms as it looks for him.

BOOP! Where did you go, you sneaky rabbit!

Now what should I do?

DO NOT ENTER!

TURN TO PAGE 58

TURN TO PAGE 136

Super Rabbit Boy swims and swims. The water starts to get shallow.

He has made it across the sea!

TURN TO PAGE 133

The animals find King Viking's hot air balloon! They jump in and fly up into the sky.

Super Rabbit Boy is almost at the factory door. The robots have not spotted him.

TURN TO PAGE 6

TURN TO PAGE 31

Super Rabbit Boy is at the base of Mount Boom.

Super Rabbit Boy tries to use his Super Jump again. But the Robo-Boss grabs him.

GAME OVER!
TURN TO PAGE 126 TO TRY AGAIN.

Super Rabbit Boy is on the seafloor. He has found an underwater city!

Super Rabbit Boy stays hidden inside the hedge.

TURN TO PAGE 57

TURN TO PAGE 118

Super Rabbit Boy finds Maria the Mermaid in a room full of treasure!

Super Rabbit Boy climbs stairs that lead up to a doorway.

132

I can see daylight!

This must be the way out.

Super Rabbit Boy is caught in a whirlpool!
He is getting pulled down toward a hole in
the seafloor.